W9-APH-583

WITHDRAWN

smile, principessa!

by Judith Ross Enderle *and* Stephanie Jacob Gordon

Illustrated by Serena Curmi

Margaret K. McElderry Books · New York · London · Toronto · Sydney

Margaret K. McElderry Books

An imprint of Simon & Schuster Children's Publishing Division

1230 Avenue of the Americas, New York, New York 10020

Text copyright © 2007 by Judith Ross Enderle and Stephanie Jacob Gordon

Illustrations copyright © 2007 by Serena Curmi

All rights reserved, including the right of reproduction in whole or in part in any form.

Book design by Debra Sfetsios

The text for this book is set in MramorCE.

The illustrations for this book are rendered in pencil and acrylic on gray board and manipulated in PhotoShop.

Manufactured in China

10 9 8 7 6 5 4 3 2 1

Library of Congress Cataloging-in-Publication Data

Enderle, Judith Ross.

Smile, Principessa! / Judith Ross Enderle and Stephanie Jacob Gordon ;

illustrated by Serena Curmi.—1st ed.

p. cm.

Summary: A sister is jealous when her baby brother starts getting all the attention in the family photographs.

ISBN-13: 978-1-4169-1004-6 (hardcover)

ISBN-10: 1-4169-1004-2

[1. Brothers and sisters—Fiction. 2. Babies—Fiction. 3. Sibling rivalry—Fiction. 4. Photography—Fiction.] I. Gordon, Stephanie Jacob, 1940– II. Curmi, Serena, ill. III. Title.

PZ7.E6965Smi 2007

[E]—dc22

2005012761

To our Principessas—Sarah, Talya, Lily, Zoey, Hannah, and Emeline—
with love and smiles from Bubbe Stephanie and Grandma Judy
—J. R. E. and S. J. G.

To my brother, Matt, for always looking out for me
—S. C.

When Principessa Razzi was born,
Mama and Papa Razzi called her our princess bambina,
our Bina.

Papa Razzi took Bina's picture every day.

Papa took smiling pictures,

crying pictures,

eating pictures,

sleeping pictures.

Papa even took one picture of Mama Razzi changing Bina's diaper.

"No more Bina diaper-changing pictures ever,"
Mama Razzi said.

Each year Papa Razzi took a thousand pictures of Bina.

Then Bambino Pasquale was born!

Mama and Papa Razzi called him
our boy bambino,
our Bino.

His sister called him Boo Boo Bino, Peeyew Bino,
and Burpy Baby Binky Bino until . . .
Mama said, "Talk nicely or you'll have a time-out, Principessa."

No one called her Bina anymore.

Now Papa Razzi took Bino's picture every day. He took smiling pictures, crying pictures, eating pictures, sleeping pictures.

Papa even took one picture of
Mama Razzi changing Bino's diaper.
"No more Bino diaper-changing
pictures ever," Mama Razzi said.
Still, everywhere all the time, Papa
Razzi said, "Smile!"

Snap!   Snap!

Snap!

But Principessa didn't like Papa's new pictures.

Not the park pictures, where she smiled her very best smile.

Not the zoo pictures, where she smiled her very best smile.

Not the beach pictures, where she smiled her very best smile.

She especially didn't like any pictures of her holding Bino.

Principessa decided she would never smile for pictures again.

Not ever!

One morning Papa Razzi held up the newspaper.
"Look at this!" he said. "A photo contest for the boy or girl
with the most beautiful smile. I must get my camera."

"Pooey," said Principessa. Papa would take a million more pictures of Bino. Bino would win the contest. Bino would be Famous Baby Bino.

While Papa got his camera, Principessa opened her closet door. She pushed her school shoes, her cowgirl boots, and her skates out of the way.

She closed the closet
door and stood inside
her bathrobe.

When her feet got tired, Principessa sat.

When her bottom got tired, Principessa lay down.

Finally, Papa Razzi called, "Principessa!"

And Mama Razzi called, "Principessa!"

"I am not coming out to watch Papa take more Bino pictures," Principessa whispered.

or under the kitchen table,

or in the bread box,"
Papa Razzi said.

"She's not under the bed,

or behind the drapes,

or in the clothes hamper,"
Mama Razzi said.

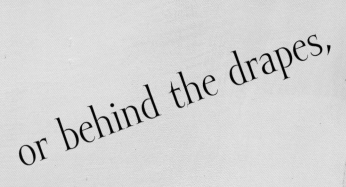

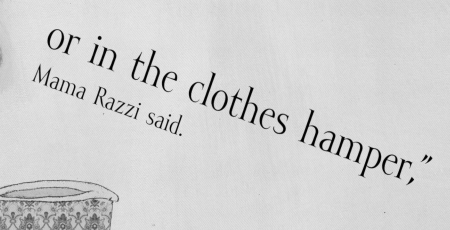

"Gurgle, gurgle, giggle, squeal,"
said Bambino Pasquale, banging the closet door.

"Where's our beautiful Principessa?" asked Mama Razzi.

Principessa made a monster face.

"That doesn't look like our beautiful Principessa," said Papa Razzi.

Principessa made a piggy face.

"Gurgle, gurgle, giggle, squeal," said Bino. *Again!*
And Bino pushed his nose flat just like Principessa.

Bino looked so funny that a tickle wiggled up inside Principessa and escaped in a giggle.

She made more faces

and so did Bino.

Finally, Principessa came out of the closet.
"Make this face, Bino," said Principessa. And for Bino she smiled

her best, most beautiful smile.

Papa Razzi took Principessa's picture.

Snap! Snap!

Snap!

Papa Razzi opened the door.
"There you are," he said. "Please
come out for the pictures."

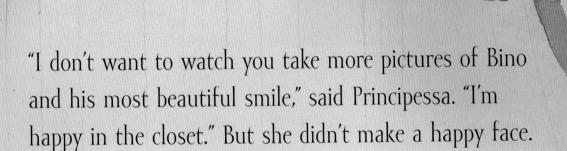

"I don't want to watch you take more pictures of Bino
and his most beautiful smile," said Principessa. "I'm
happy in the closet." But she didn't make a happy face.

"Yes, Bino has a beautiful smile," Mama Razzi said.

Papa Razzi agreed. "I have taken many baby pictures of
Bino. Just like I took many baby pictures of you. But he
is just a bambino. And you are our only princess."

Principessa still didn't come out of the closet.

"Come out
and smile, Principessa,"
said Papa Razzi.

Principessa sat under her bathrobe
and made a grumpy witch face.

3 1491 00961 4474

Niles
Public Library District
JAN 0 9 2008
Niles, Illinois 60714